The crooked chefs

Revealing the truth how chefs and
managers earn their money the
crooked way at their bosses expenses.

Marco Moreli

www.newgeneration-publishing.com

 **New Generation Publishing**

Introduction

This book is about you learning to pick up a pan or knife or providing new methods for cooking or even teaching you how to cook. This book reveals the truth about chefs and the depth of how their knowledge about running their kitchens. It reveals how your books can be cooked by the people you trust to run your kitchen for you. How their devious manners can ruin hotels restaurants etc. It can't be said that all chefs of all levels are combined in the one pot of stew or trying to cook your pockets the same. Never before has any chef wanted to expose and open that can that will allow all the worms out. Maybe one of the reasons for not wanting to do so is guilt. Guilt of abusing the foundations the love and the passion for cooking.

I hope you enjoy this edition.

Starting off looking out for a part time job to keep myself day to day I came upon a place which displayed a notice for staff wanted in the window. I went in and asked to speak with the kitchen manager. I was asked if I was looking for a floor job and I replied no I was looking for a kitchen job and would it be possible for me to talk with a member of the senior kitchen staff or manager. After about 20 minutes of waiting a small man in a white uniform appeared and asked what he could do for me. I asked him if he had any kitchen jobs available. He spoke in a very polite manner and said he could offer me a pot and wash job which meant washing and cleaning of pots and kitchen utensils. He said it would be a hard and tough job. I accepted his offer as I needed some kind of income.

True to his word it was a hard and tough going job. I started in the November. My first impression of this kitchen was it was very hot and intense, lots of shouting, screaming, swearing, things been thrown, basically just mayhem. I thought to myself the best thing I can do is just get stuck in and get on with it. With that the second chef in command came to me and shouts 'hey young man put this uniform on and start peeling these potatoes'. When I seen and realized the amount of potatoes he had left for me to peel I thought to myself oh no this is something I really don't want to do but knew I had to if I wanted to keep my job. Up to that I had been enjoying my space in my little pot wash room. I was taken aside and shown how to peel potatoes and vegetables of all sorts. I remained doing this job for several months and during this time encountered good and bad times, but mainly what stuck out in my mind was, the sheer malice, deception and badness that went on between chefs. It was on a high level everyday and often made working conditions intolerable. Eventually I became intolerant to the atmosphere and knew it was time to move on.

Almost straight away I landed myself a job in a restaurant which was owned by a very kind man who was also the chef. He was a pure and devoted Christian and made me feel very welcome and at home right from the start. The rest of the staff were also very friendly and made me feel part of their team. Very quickly I established the chef was a man with very high standards of experience and credentials. He was a true chef in every sense of the word. He was honest, dedicated proud and held very good leadership skills. Even on a personal level outside work he was a pure gentleman. He invited to me

Church held occasions and even invited me to his home to spend Christmas with him and his family two years in a row. He thought me so much on a personal level and working level. To this day I hold the highest respect for this man. I stayed working with him for almost two years. To the shock of everybody the man became very sick after suffering a brain haemorrhage. He remained in hospital for a long period of time and felt he could no longer carry on with his business. Unfortunately we all had to move on and find new jobs. My career as a chef took off very successfully and led me to places where I learned from the best and was very grateful to deserve being called 'a good chef'.

Thieving

This is when and where my eyes started to open to the true goings on of chefs and kitchens. From now on, this is where all my information and facts arise from and the reason for me writing this book in the first place. I have worked along side well known celebrity chefs, with amazing talents, competent passionate chefs, with full focus and direction in their jobs. These are the people who are deserving of the title chef. Unfortunately this kind is very far and few between. We have the cowboys, unfortunately who come in higher numbers than the real chefs. There are so many of them out there claiming to be 'good chefs' which realistically they are no more than thieves without the masks and wearing white uniforms. They put on a good show of pretending to know what they are actually doing while their main concern is cooking your dough well for their own benefits and interests. These so called chefs are very good at building up their curriculum vitae when applying for jobs claiming to have worked in places that they never did or winning medals or awards for their outstanding culinary skills. Far too many employers fall in to their trap by believing the impressive show the cowboy had just put on. By the time they realize what has been really going on its too late. This can lead to owners being thrown in to deep debt or even worse having to close their doors which has happened to a number of establishments.

I remember working in a particular place where the chef was robbing as much as possible from the kitchen ranging from meat to dry goods, I mean anything he could possibly manage. He would sneak the stuff down to the basement and in to a bag he would have already had down there. I am talking about hundreds of euro worth not just small amounts. One day when he discovered I had seen what he was at, he threatened me that if I opened my mouth he would have my legs broken for me. Eventually some one else copped on to his tricks and he ended up being fired for his behaviours. He at the time blamed me for his downfall but greed was actually his downfall not me. The more he got away with the bigger and better he would do the next time. The downfall of hotels and restaurants is nearly always down to the bad running or creaming off profits by the chefs or kitchen staff. Head chefs and managers have the duty to make sure things are running smoothly and making the most of supplies and stock they have at hand. A lot of chefs and managers work hand in hand together to make as much profits for themselves as possible. When a chef especially a head chef applies for a job and comes to their interview most managers want to sit in on the interview so they work out if this person will be willing to fit in to the circle of deception and thievery. If he gets the vibes that this person is of the same ideas as himself he nearly almost be guaranteed to get the job as the manager will highly recommend him to the owner. If the opposite happens and he feels the applicant seems to be straight down the line and honest, whether or not he is an excellent chef or not he will most probably not get the job because the manager will find some other fault with him to undo the good impression the applicant was trying to make on the owner. It is a very tight knit circle between managers, chefs and suppliers. The manager knows he needs a crooked chef to play ball with bribing suppliers so he and the head chef are sure of their monthly backhanders. I have witnessed this so many times with suppliers, here is an example of one such time. I was working for a man who I had the highest respect for, he was a very fair, fun loving character who was very family orientated. He always made sure his staff were well looked after and he took interest in the people that worked for him. When one day a local butcher came in and introduced himself to me. As we were chatting he handed me a . When one day a local butcher came in and introduced himself to me. As we were chatting he handed me a 50 pound note, very confused I asked him what it was for and he replied it was no problem I always reward chefs that were willing to look after me giving me good frequent business, the more they order from me the more he rewards. He was basically bribing me. I thought this was fierce insulting to me and the owner who was decent enough to pay this butcher in full on or before the due date. I put the money in the office drawer and went about weighing the meat he had just delivered. I can still to this day remember what it was he brought, they were boned and rolled legs of lamb and when I put them on my kitchen scales they were a lot more under weight than what was ordered and of very poor quality I mean the meat bloody meat was just starting to turn grey. When I approached him and told him I wasn't happy about thee quality and it being underweight he just smiled at me and said 'well there you go do you catch my drift'. Actually what he meant was no matter what he was going to bring in the future despite the quality or weight of it I was just to accept it and sign the docket for it say nothing and I would get my reward from him at the end of the month. I was left standing totally shocked with what had just taken place. Straight away I went upstairs to the owners office and told him of the goings on I had just encountered, and how the butcher had implied he paid all the previous head chefs off in return for bigger business and supplying substandard meat. Without hesitation or a word to me he picked up the phone and what he didn't say to this man wasn't worth saying, needless to say we never seen that butchers face around again. My point is it so handy to make extra cash for yourself as a head chef if you are that way inclined, but if an owner is willing to look after you well in return for you to do a good job and he puts his trust in you, why would you want to rip him off and risk the chance of getting fired and ruining your reputation, as word gets around very quickly between chefs in different establishments.

Another good example of this is when I went to work in a big hotel in the midlands as a second chef (sous chef), as I had been asked to help out reshaping the kitchen and provide help to the head chef. To my surprise as I walked in to the kitchen to be introduced to such a young head chef for whom I knew for his age couldn't have had the experience necessary to hold the position of head chef. I was taken aback that for a hotel with a good reputation that they would have given charge of their food side of business to him. I said nothing and just started to get on with my duties when the assistant manager a little guy, again very young came to me and suggested we should have a chat on how to improve the quality of the food and the direction the hotel should follow. He signaled to me that he felt the head chef should stand down from his position as he lacked experience and ability to run a kitchen and cook the standard of food the hotel owner expected. I knew the head chef was a personal good friend of the manager and was totally shocked he was back stabbing him and speaking and making little of him to me. As we were chatting I mentioned to him that a delivery had arrived earlier. It was from a cash and carry and consisted of dry goods and the bill came to around 2600 euro. I wondered why so much had been ordered, when there was already still large amounts of stock there. When I said to him that all this stock ordered was not needed he told me it was ok that it would be used for the weekend. I brought it to his attention that the week wasn't going to be as busy as he might have thought. He purely dismissed what I had just said and told me just to let it go. I soon realized the head chef didn't have the authority to do the ordering of stock and it was the stock controller and assistant manager that were doing the ordering. As time was going on I was amazed of the quantity of the food that was being thrown in to the bin and when I told the assistant manager, again his answer was 'we can afford to throw it in the bin' he was simply telling me to back off and mind my own business. It was really obvious from that moment what was going on. The staff had been hand picked to fit in to the circle of deception and thievery which I mentioned before. From the young head chef who couldn't cook or run a kitchen, the assistant manager who had no costings plan or profit margins or experience to the general manager who simply just didn't want to know. It was just basically a money making scheme between themselves without a thought for the owner. When they realized I was not willing to fit in to their circle and turn a blind eye they made it difficult for me so I would leave of my own accord. Eventually I did. I couldn't stand by and watch, signing for deliveries that didn't even come through the door.

Another making scheme chefs have is to con or persuade owners that the kitchen is in need of updating and in need of new equipment. They will convince him that the equipment they are using is no good and will go to any lengths to get as much new stuff as they can, ranging from small items to larger ones such as cookers and high cost items, because already they would have a supplier for such equipment lined up to supply and install the un needed money wasted equipment. The supplier will quote a price to either the chef or manager and then give a substantially higher one to the owner making sure that they will make a nice profit from the deal behind the owners back. It is an unbelievable story how big establishments can be brought down by staff. If the establishment has a bar chefs will recruit bar staff during the day providing them with good standard meals then the bar staff will return the favour to him at night by giving him a free bar for the night for him and his friends or family so by this time the owner has been ripped of on the double.

One night we had just finished service for a wedding reception myself and a few other kitchen staff went out the back yard for a quick cup of coffee we noticed two young bar men with black sacks placing them in the boot of the bar managers car. It was a bit unusual. We approached them and as we did we could hear rattling of bottles coming from the bags. They were full if bottles of vodka, whiskey, brandy, wine and other spirits. I asked what were they doing and they said they have been told to bring these to the car and they said nothing else they were just following orders. I then went to the bar manager and asked him the same question and he told me that he was returning them to another establishment that he had borrowed them from previously. I thought this was a bit odd firstly bringing them at that hour of the night and secondly this big hotel were we were working would not have let stock run down that lot especially when they were catering for a big wedding that weekend. It turned out the owner had his suspicions about the stock taker that controlled the stock for the bar and disco but had never had enough proof on him stealing the stock. A few of his family members were also working in the hotel at the time too, but they realized it wouldn't be safe for them to harbor the stolen stock just in case major suspicion arose around the stock controller or any of his family members as this would be the first place and the first people they would check so he cleverly recruited the bar manager on his side. Am sure the bar manager didn't need much persuading as he knew he would get his cut from the sale of the stolen goods. I knew there would be no point in me saying anything as they would all have angles covered if they were caught and very well rehearsed story and after all I was not part of their staff I was kitchen staff. I knew it would just be a matter of time when they slipped up and would walk themselves into trouble, sure enough a couple of weeks later the boss was upstairs in the office where the monitors for the highly sophisticated cameras were placed and noticed goings on in the yard at the rear of the hotel. When he zoomed the cameras in he could see two people bundling boxes into a wheelie bin. He immediately went down to the yard to find the bar manager and the stock controller trying to cover up the boxes they had just placed in the bin with cardboard. The boss opened the bin to find boxes of unopened boxes of whiskey and Bacardi. They were fired on the spot, god only knows how much they had stolen in the past and the value of it. I really don't understand how any staff member can degrade themselves so badly just for a few quid, these kind of crooked chefs managers and bar staff all assume that the owner is financially well off and can afford to be stolen from, little do they know some owners are struggling to keep their heads above water too.

Hygiene

Personal hygiene among a lot of chefs is pure shocking. You will find quite a number of them working in uniforms that are supposed to be white, but look more like they have just finished washing the floor with them. After having a busy day and night it is quite obvious chefs will smell of food, fish especially holds a strong smell on uniforms and skin, but is disturbing to come in to work the following day to find chefs you worked with the previous day still smelling of the same smell as the night before where it becomes obvious they have not showered or changed their clothes. Long hair should always be tied up under a hat or hair net but it is uncommon to find chefs working with hair hanging hair hanging loosely and uncovered. Clean or unclean hair should never be on display. Now you can imagine the chefs that don't shower and change their clothes, I am sure they don't make any exception for their hair. Even the thought of it sounds vile.

I recall working in this particular place where the head chef was absolutely filthy. He would go to the bathroom and return to cooking without even washing his hands. He would stand with his hands down his trousers scratching, or picking his uncut fingernails. One evening during service a waiter came in to the kitchen with a plate being returned by a customer, it was a fish dish, the waiter said the costumer had complained that the fish smelled off and wanted a replacement one. To my astonishment the head chef took the same fish from the plate spit on it, then smothers it with plain white sauce an squeezes some lemon on it and places it under the grill for a few minutes puts it on a new plate, places a bit of parsley on top and sends it back out to the costumer. My stomach was turning watching him never mind the poor costumer that was going to receive it. Again the waiter came in with the same smelly fish and wanted chicken instead. The head chef replied I will give the p***k chicken to remember, with that he took a fillet of chicken from the fridge dipped it in the wash up sink which was full of dirty greasy water and threw it on to the griddle in pure frustration and anger. When it was cooked he dressed it up and told the waiter to tell the costumer that the chef said he hopes he enjoys his meal. This is a head chef who is supposed to be showing an example and leadership to the junior chefs. This lad served some rubbish in his time but used to take home with him some of the freshest expensive prime steak, fish and whatever he fancied. In many an establishment I have witnessed chefs dropping meat or other foods on the floor and picking them straight back up and carry on as if nothing happened. First off that meat or whatever it was that fell on the floor is now covered in bacteria ready to be served to an unsuspecting customer. Apart from being so unhygienic themselves they are putting costumers at risk. I have seen food returned by costumers being dipped in bins, stepped on, spat on and many other disgusting things been done to it before it is sent back out to the paying costumer. I will now tell you of kitchens that are run by chefs that wouldn't have an idea what haccp means. The kitchens are so dirty that they are a health risk. Unfortunately I can not reveal the names of places and names of chefs involved in this despicable behaviour. This particular hotel had a very large kitchen and was very well equipped with fridges and freezers and whatever else was needed to ensure a high standard of hygiene but it was abused by the head chef in charge. He would take deliveries of dry goods and throw them on the floor then another delivery of meat would arrive and he would throw that on the floor beside the dry goods and other deliveries that might arrive such as fruit and veg. straight away cross contamination is taken place before it even reaches fridges or shelves. His filthy and unhygienic habits were rubbing off the junior chefs and kitchen porters as they wouldn't take any responsibility to organise and separate the different deliveries. After all you can not really put blame with them, because if a man who is supposed to be your leader and inspiration doesn't care why the hell should a junior chef?. If haccp is not followed properly it can lead to wither food poisoning or could result in closure of your establishment. These are just some of the ways that can lead to cross contamination and food poisoning. As I already told you about the bad hygiene and habits of these crooked chefs this is only the start of it. I once had the experience of opening a fridge to find meat stored on the top shelf beside the likes of dairy products, the blood dripping from the meats down on top of the uncovered items in the fridge. The inside of the fridge itself was filthy and had crusted blood and sauces on the shelving which had been spilt and never cleaned up, and I can tell you judging from the smell this didn't happen either today or yesterday it had to be there for at least a couple of weeks.

There was fungus growing on the back wall of the interior of the fridge. Just imagine the amount of germs and bacteria that were having a field day in there. Also the fridge was set at wrong temperature, other big problem. Each type of food should have its own colour chopping board. Far too often the same board is been used for fish, meat, veg, raw and cooked foods without ever been cleaned after each use. A lot of the time veg is not washed before being used. I recall one time I was preparing a warmed goat's cheese salad and I asked the commis chef to wash lettuce for me and arrange it on to a plate. Just as I went to place the warmed goat's cheese on top of the salad I spotted a slug in between the leaves. In pure disgust I called him over and showed him what I had just found, his best idea was to pick the slug out and just carry on. I got so angry with him asking how the hell a slug was in the lettuce if he had just washed it. He calmly replied I didn't wash it as the previous chef told me, if I didn't see any dirt or soil on it not to bother washing it as it was just a waste of time. If I hadn't have noticed the slug that dish would have been served to a costumer. I guarantee you would not have seen that costumer in the establishment again and they would have bad mouthed it to other people. In reality who would actually blame them, I have seen meat been put into an oven which wouldn't be turned o to make space on counters, but the oven still would be warm from previous use, so the meat is been heated mildly and maybe taken back out and put back into a fridge, this is a walking ground for bacteria. Chicken being taken from the freezer and being defrosted quickly on high power in microwave to speed things up but again a walking ground for bacteria. I could go on and on about this kind of disgusting and hazardous behaviour but I think by now you have a fairly good idea of what I am talking about. Again I must stress as I have done before all chefs are not the same, if you look hard enough you will find the respectable, honest, hardworking, clean hygienic ones who can actually cook. None of the shocking but true facts I have written about so far can ever lead to a successful profitable business for the owner or a hygienic setting for the customer. After all it's the customer that any establishment depends on, and if the staff running it are anything like what I have described what chance does it stand. Honestly put yourself in the shoes of the customer dining in these kinds of places I have described and if you had any idea of what goes on behind the scenes in the kitchen would you accept the food you were being served or better still would you even go to that place at all. I bet you wouldn't and you would make sure anybody else you knew wouldn't go there either. That's how so many establishments go down hill. Restaurants reputations depend on customer satisfaction, if a customer has a bad experience they will quite rightly spread the word and soon bookings will keep dropping until it comes you have almost no bookings at all, but the owner still has to pay staff to be there just incase in the remote chance somebody might walk through the door that hasn't heard of the bad reputation that the place holds. The owner is at loss again. On the other hand if a restaurant has a good reputation word will travel very quickly on this too. There a quite a lot of people who dine out a lot and get to know what is expected of a fine restaurant, if they choose to dine in your restaurant and are pleased with the food ambiance and service you can be guaranteed they will return again maybe bringing more people with them the next time, or even pass the good word around on how much they enjoyed their evening. Good word of mouth is always the best kind of advertisement a restaurant can put out there.

Bad attitudes among chefs

Chefs have to be the most temperamental people you will ever come across. Kitchens become very heated in two ways, temperatures from cookers ovens etc, but the worst heat is the heat from the soaring tempers of the chefs. Some of the so called head chefs that parade around the kitchen doing actually no work what so ever displaying their medals they have supposedly won in the past as I would like to call them 'their medals of honour'. What a f*****g joke. On a busy night in service the last thing you want to know about or see is this assholes medals, you just want them to get their finger out of where ever he had it stuck and get stuck in helping to get the service out as quickly and professionally as possible. Unfortunately there are so many that want to hide away in the back round while its busy and are not concerned about earning their wage honestly from hard work. This will automatically drive the rest of the chefs mad who are giving a hundred per cent dedication to what they are doing and the walk around head chef will take all the glory at the end of the night if the service ran smoothly. Tempers start to run wild at this kind of carry on and the other chefs feel they cant say anything to the head chef so they all end up arguing and shouting among themselves, and then the whole communication process breaks down between them and then things start to go wrong. Instead of this medallion man (head chef) showing leadership and authority in his kitchen he is actually the cause of the mayhem taking place. I remember one time a junior chef was running the kitchen like a possessed lunatic during a busy night, as the head chef stood by and watched, I knew it was only going to be a matter of time before disaster struck, when I heard this unmerciful scream. The young chef had slipped, dipping his hand in to scalding oil in the fryer, he jumped back in shock smashing in to another chef that was carrying a hot tray he had just taken from the oven causing the tray to crash in to his chest. All again lack of leadership and team work two people ended up going to hospital that night. On the other hand you will get chefs who abuse their authorities and undermine the junior chefs and kitchen porters,they think the only way they can communicate is to shout and scream at the top of their voices, little do they know this is when everybody loses respect for them. If a chef genuinely makes a mistake there is no need to shout and scream at them and degrade them in front of the other staff. The best thing the head chef or senior chef should do is point out where and how the mistake was made and how to rectify it. A lot of the chefs think that lower experienced staff such as commis chefs or kitchen porters are like something they have just scraped off the end of their shoe and treat them like it too. There was once a man in his fifties who earned and deserved his wage through washing pots and kitchen untensils. As any kitchen worker well knows this is not a very pleasant job to do. It was made particularly horrible for him by this self over rated chef who would just throw the pots or whatever in his direction to wash and demand them back clean in a matter of minutes. I never once heard him ask this man in a polite or dignified tone of voice to do anything just spoke to him every time in a vile and degrading manner. One night after we had finished work I got talking to the middle aged man, I found him to be a well educated man and he held a lot of worldly experience. He was a very interesting man. I asked him how he could stand for a young, still green behind the ears chef to put him down and degrade him day after day in front of the rest of the staff, he replied 'lad life doesn't always pan out the way we plan it and some times at some part of our lives we have to do things we really don't want to do and unfortunately this is my time'. He said he needed to earn money and at his age it was difficult to find work as he had been made redundant from his previous job. All he wanted to do was to go to work do the job he was being paid to do and go home and at the end of the week pick up his wages. Nobody actually wants to choose this as their line of work but they still deserve the right of respect from their co-workers. A few days later I couldn't allow myself to let this chef get away with treating the man like a piece of s**t anymore. I asked him who the hell he thought he thought he was talking to a man of his age the way he did, and degrading him and making his job harder than it had to be. This low grade of a chef turned to me and asked me why I was so bothered about an auld lad who was willing to wash pots for a living. I was fuming with him at this stage and asked him how he would feel if it was his father been treated like that by some other little p***k in his job, making it clear to him that this man didn't want to be here and unlike him was willing to do the job he was being paid to do and was deserving of his wage he was handed at the end of the week. At least this man could walk away at the end of the day with his head held high with pride knowing that he had done his job well. How many chefs can honestly say that. Junior chefs will learn from good senior chefs if they are given the opportunity to do so. They will make mistakes along the way as we all do. Most of the senior chefs couldn't be bothered to show them how to create a dish or the techniques to help them progress in their careers, this can often be down to them not really knowing how to cook themselves and others are afraid that this young chef might flourish in to a good chef and show the senior chef up or better still end up taking his job. Every head chef started from scratch they didn't just first time off land a ahead chef job but they seem to forget this. Without them been giving a chance by whoever they were trained by they wouldn't be where they are today although in some cases that wouldn't be a bad thing. As I started off doing the same job as the middle aged man and worked my way up the ranks I learned to be respectful to all levels of kitchen staff as I had at some time in the past held the same position as them and I wanted to be treated with respect when I was at their stage. I also learned that senior ranks above you needed to be respected too as they had worked hard to get where they were, (I am talking about the ones who deserved to be respected and those who were worthy of being there).

Now a days chefs think they have the most stressful pressurized jobs in the world. They portray themselves as martyrs to the cooking cause. So many of them turn to either drink or worse again taking drugs. This is just an excuse to let their true inner self out. I have seen too many of them turning up to work either under the influence of alcohol or drugs. They will slip out on their break to take what ever it is they take. As soon as they are finished work they will head straight for the bar. I know so many chefs who are hooked on cocaine. A chef came in one day and I knew by the way he was joking and messing about that he had just taken something. On getting closer to him I noticed his eyes were shiny and glossy, he was hyper but I didn't have any real proof to accuse him. We got on with the days work and as it was his last shift because he had just come in part time I said nothing. All the kitchen staff decided to go for a drink that night to mark his last day and Christmas was approaching I agreed to go along.

The night was going great until he came over to me and a few others and blatantly offered us cocaine. We were all shocked at that he was so casual in doing so, like he was offering us a sweet or something. He claimed it took the edge off the shitty job he was doing, and it helped him to chill out. He was totally out of order. I don't understand. As the saying goes 'if you cant stand the heat stay out of the kitchen'. Why do they choose to be chefs in the first place if they are just going to use it as an excuse to abuse alcohol or drugs. Being around or working with some one under the influence of a substance or recovering from the night before is almost impossible to get a days work done as they cannot concentrate on what they are doing, making mistakes which slows the whole service down or even worse be a danger to those around them. I came across a lad who spent almost his entire wages on cocaine so you can imagine what type of hygiene he had or what his ability to work was like, but a blind eye was turned because he fit in to the circle I spoke about before, the circle of deception and thievery.

Trust between chefs is nearly almost an alien word. They are the most back stabbing bunch imaginable. On taking over the head chef position in this particular hotel, I wanted to build up a good strong kitchen team so I recruited chefs, some I had known for years, one was even my best mate. Most of them were either unhappy in their previous employment and some of them were not even employed at the time. I took on this couple who were good friends of mine. She was a pastry chef with whom I had worked with before and she seemed hardworking and good at her job. I promoted her husband as my right hand man. I put my trust in to them trusting their judgements, loyalty and capability to work along side me as we had done before. The couple had been struggling to pay a mortgage on a new house they had just built and were finding it hard to find suitable jobs paying enough money or matching shits allowing them to spend time together as they were only newly weds. That's what made me give them the jobs in the first place as everybody wants to help a friend out, well that's what I thought. Very soon I would learn different. As time went on I noticed changes in them all. Little did I know they were slicing and carving my back to the boss. The one that I had given the position to as my right hand man was planning to take over my position all along and bring his wife and my so called mate who by now I had found out was a pure alcoholic with him on the ride. They concocted stories about me between them and served them nicely to the boss. It totally sickened my stomach to see how through greed and dishonesty, my so called mates were stabbing me in the back all along. I left soon after to take up a position elsewhere. I later heard my so called right hand man had taken over the kitchen, serving pure muck to customers. His idea of fine dining was serving burgers. His wife was taking ecstasy tablets which she had done in the past but told me she was off them when I employed her to work along side me. Between his inability to cook and her drug taking the kitchen was being literally run in to the ground. The level of hygiene got so bad that the health inspector came in and gave them a couple of days to sort out the filth and mess in the kitchen. This was a real blow to such a well known hotel. The couple were slowly pushed out by the owners and then my so called alcoholic mate left too. The owners then took back control of the kitchen. One day as I was working in my new job I got a phone call from the owners asking me would I consider going back as head chef as they had made a mistake trusting and listening to the other bunch of cowboys, and they had later realized that I had been stabbed in the back all the way. I declined their offer as I was happy where I was and didn't feel the vibe to go back. So there you have it, you try to help some one out and you end up being slowly boiled by them.

Once we were preparing for a wedding in this place I instructed a chef to take charge of cooking beef, telling him how long it had to stay in the oven and even the exact temperature and what time the meat was needed for, as it would need to rest for a while before carving. He got on with what I had instructed so I left him alone as he was a well experienced chef. The time came to take the meat out of the oven when e came to me with a worried look on his face and said, 'chef I forgot to turn the oven on' at this point I really thought he was having me on playing a joke on me, but when his expression didn't change I realized he was serious. He failed to see the huge disaster he had just brought upon us. He hadn't got a clue what was about to happen. While this was taking place in the kitchen the waiting staff were out on the floor taking orders from the wedding party. We had to intervene and ask them to slow down the process as much as possible in order to make up time to cook the beef. It was a pure disaster. All I could think about was the couple who were paying thousands for their wedding and we having to slow down their meal service all because of one so called chef who couldn't even manage to turn on the oven. Another muppet like him decided to serve almost raw chicken fillets to the carvery, imagine this guy had been cooking for over 30 years and still couldn't tell the difference between raw and cooked chicken. What he had done was to seal off the chicken and finish cooking them in the alto sham (a compartment designed to keep food warm after it has been fully cooked) and any half decent chef should know this, its not designed for cooking food as it hasn't enough strength and power to do so.

In 2001 I opened my first restaurant and was very ambitious to make it work. After a year of working seven days a week I decided to take a short break away with my wife and kids. All it was for was four days. I called on a chef friend asking him would he be willing to cover my few days away. He said he would be delighted and honoured to do it. I went through the whole run down of the place with him and was willing to pay him a good wage for his time. The excitement was unreal. The day finally came for me head off, we had arranged for him to be at the restaurant at 10am for me to hand him over the keys. 10am passed and I thought he must be held up, 11am still no sign so I decided to ring him. His phone rang out without answer. Again and again I rang still now answer. It was 1pm by now so I knew something wasn't right, he never did answer his phone that day. So there was no short holiday, and having to tell my family was not very pleasant, but what annoyed and disgusted me the most was his blatant unworthiness and dishonor. He wasn't even man enough to let me know a day or two before hand. To this day I have not heard from or seen him. A huge percentage of chefs cannot be trusted both in work or in personal aspects. Its amazing how many sick chefs you will find on a Friday or saturday night as they do not want to work on these nights they want to be out socializing. You can almost sense when the phone is going to ring with one of them on the other end getting ready to tell you their sob story of how sick they are and you know they are no more sick than you are. They have no consideration how the rest of the kitchen is going to manage without cover for the missing one, their socializing is priority to them. I recall one time when we had a very busy weekend ahead of us with two weddings to cater for one on the Friday and the other on the Saturday. On the Thursday of the same week one of the chefs came in and told me he was handing in his notice and would not be working after that day. He said he would not be working out his notice as he had another job to go to on the Monday of the following week, I asked him would he consider staying until the Saturday night until we had the two weddings covered almost coming to the stage of begging him, but he said no he wanted to enjoy his weekend off before starting his new job on the Monday. That was leaving the rest of us under severe pressure to cater for these two weddings with one of the senior chefs missing. The Friday came and we were preparing for the wedding when the phone rang at half past nine in the morning, again it was another chef claiming to be sick, I told him there was no way he could take these two days off as we were already one man down and under staffed as it was but he insisted he was too sick and would not be able to work. I was left in deep s**t, having to ring around other chefs I knew to see if they would be willing to work with us knowing in my heart that this was going to be difficult as in every hotel and restaurant they would all be working Friday and Saturday nights themselves. One very decent lad obliged me to work from ten thirty until three thirty on both days as he started his own shift at four on these days. Without his help we would never have got the job done properly. He was that decent he wouldn't even accept any payment and told me maybe some day he would be in the same position and could rely on me to do the same for him. He is one of the rare good chefs that deserved the title 'chef'. After finishing work on the Saturday night totally wrecked I was driving home and who did I see only the very sick chef falling out of the pub drunk with his mates laughing and joking. This is what I mean when I say chefs have no loyalty to their work or co-workers. On the Monday when he did arrive to work I told him what I had seen on the Saturday night, but he tried to convince me I was mistaken and he was at home in bed very sick. Apart from his disloyal behaviour and his lying he was now trying to insult my intelligence which really boiled my blood. He done this so often at the weekends he was fired for it after been giving prior warnings. Everybody has days when they feel like not wanting to go to work but anyone who has respect for their job, their bosses and co-workers and most important themselves will just get on with it and do it anyway rather than letting so many people down, but unfortunately 90% of chefs don't fall in to this catergory.

Restaurant and hotel owners falling in to debt

Restaurant and hotel owners are falling in to debt every day and not through fault of their own, but by being fleeced by their kitchen staff. I came across this young entrepreneur who comes from a very respectful family. He open his pub then after that expanded to the restaurant side of it. This pub had been in his family for generations and he rebuilt it again from scratch. Hen he decided to open the restaurant part of it, he hired a chef who had convinced she was the right woman for the job. Things were going well for a while until she started to dictate the whole show and not giving the owner a say in anything that went on in his own restaurant. After a few months things went from bad to worse. He found for the amount of food been produced and sold things were not adding up on the financial side. The supplier bills were mounting up dramatically and at the end of the month there was no profit been made. This went on for a while until one day he found himself actually getting in to debt and pumping money from the pub in to the kitchen to try and keep it afloat. He really couldn't understand how he was losing so much. The chef started to make more problems for him by refusing to cook after a certain time. After all if a customer enters your doors a few minutes after the last order time it is very unprofessional to turn them away. After you are finished your last order and while you are cleaning your kitchen it is common practice for any good chefs to leave their oven cookers and fryers on in the event of a late comer. When the owner suggested this to her she became very abusive, yelling and screaming at him.

Anyway that was just the tip of the iceberg. He now finds himself being conned by the chef and her having a laugh at his expense. Things got so out of hand he took the decision to let her go. He rang me one day and asked would I be able to help him out for a couple of weeks, to try and sort out the mess she had left behind. I had my own job at the time but obliged to do it in between my own working hours. When I went to check the kitchen out I was astonished by my findings. The fridges, freezers dry goods storage were over packed with food. Fish, chicken, meat, desserts, I could go on and fill three pages listing the amount of food in the kitchen. Most of it was ordered unnecessarily. She was ordering the most expensive items from the most expensive suppliers,you might ask why would she want to do that but as I told you before about the suppliers that reward the chef at the end of the month, and the more expensive the order the bigger the reward would be. She was lining her pockets at the owners expense. The poor b*****d was fighting to survive. I stepped in and took control of the mess and tried to make, even the money he had spent on the food back for him. It took about seven months before he had space to breath again, he could finally see light at the end of the tunnel, between the outstanding bills, things start turning around for him. Things were finally starting to run well for him when one day he received a registered letter. On opening it he found he found it to be a court order for the unfair dismissals court. It's the very same chef that he had no choice but to let go who was bringing him to an unfair dismissal tribunal, and demanding a few thousand euro from him. I mean what the f**k is this world coming to, she rips him off leaving him in major debt and dire straits then adds salt to the wound by bringing him to the unfair dismissals court. It was her incompetence and greed that landed her where she was. I know this guy very well, he is a very fair and honest guy, who is always willing to help anyone out when ever or however he can. This kind of story is unfortunately not an uncommon one, it has happened to so many restaurant and hotel owners. Hopefully by reading this book it will stop anymore trusting owners falling in to the devious claws of these low grade kind of chefs. My biggest hope is that this book will expose all the under world type of carry on that goes on in kitchens forcing the crooked chefs out of the cooking business altogether. Any decent respectful honest chef reading this book knows they have nothing to worry about, it will only be the crooked ones that will lie in fear of being discovered by their boss as been of low grade, thieving from him losing him business through bad hygiene and all the other aspects I have mentioned in previous chapters. At the end of the day it will always be the owner who is at loss and will come out the worst of the wear when the s**t hits the fan. These low grade crooked chefs, managers, stock controllers and who ever else they have in their circle of deception and thievery have already built themselves a nice little package both from the wage you have paid them and by the special monthly rewards he has being receiving from the crooked suppliers off your back. You will be amazed how much has been going on behind your back and under your nose that you had no clue about, while these people are smiling to your face and when you turn your back are stabbing you in the back and thieving from your pockets.

How restaurants and hotels can fail

Its amazing how many restaurant and hotel owners have not got a clue how their chefs and managers are ripping them off on a daily basis. They don't suspect anything as they put their trust in to the people they have appointed to run their business for them. I am hoping any owner reading this will find it helpful and that it gives them a good insight how to keep a close eye on what is really going on in their kitchens and keep their business running profitable and not fall in to the claws of the crooked chefs and managers.

First off I recommend when any senior chef or manager initially applies for a job that you fully check out their references and do some homework on them before appointing them. Its important to know what experience they really hold and why they finished in their last job. You can find out a lot by telephoning their previous employers or referees they have supplied on their curriculum vitae. The attitude of the referee towards the person can very often give you a good insight in to their attitude to work. Its time worth spending checking them out before its too late.. Any decent honest chef or manager wont mind you checking out their references or phoning their previous employers but if you do sense some hesitation you know there is something that they don't want exposed about them, so straight off that should set off alarms for you. If from the off you feel any sort of bad vibe coming from them trust your instincts instantly as these crooked chefs and managers are skilled craftsmen on how to mould and bend staff and owners in to what ever shape they need. If you feel uncomfortable with the applicant never put your full trust in to them straight away or the full running of your business as don't forget these are still strangers to you. It helps if you can spare time regularly each week to make your presence known as they will never know when it is safe to do their dirty tricks and if you can flexi the times you are there. This will make them more nervous about even thinking about bending the rules. If a head chef or manager tries to cut you out of any financial decision concerning their domain I would make it clear to them you want to know about any new suppliers they are dealing with or any new equipment to be ordered has to be run by you first. At all times crooked chefs have their own line of suppliers ready from the off as soon as they are appointed and as I explained before about the circle of deception and thievery, these will be suppliers who hand out rewards to the chefs at the end of the month in return for large expensive orders. I know its not always feasible to check every order or every delivery in big establishments but it is advisable to check weekly bookings list against orders been made. You will know if it's a busy week understandably suppliers orders will be relatively high and on the other hand if bookings are low orders should be of a normal rate. If a head chef or manager insists on using certain suppliers its well worth your while shopping around different suppliers for price lists and compare prices to the one your chef is using. If there is a considerable difference to the higher with the chefs choice then there is definitely cause for concern.

When the head chef needs a sous chef or any other senior chef its very advisable that if possible you can appoint these yourself independently to the head chef or manager as this strips away any corrupt ideas they might have had about finding the right type of chef to fit in to their circle. If this is not possible then you should always make sure you can sit in on interviews and don't be influenced by the head chefs or managers decisions always trust your own instincts. Any head chef or manager who has nothing to hide and is honest will appreciate your involvement. Most employers find interviews boring and tiresome but don't forget these are people who have your business in their hands, and you have only just met them. You wouldn't hand over your cheque book or bank card to people you don't know and trust, but its from their honesty that you will learn to trust them and feel safe to give the majority, never the full responsibility for them to run your business.

Another aspect is to pass through your kitchen regularly to see for yourself the level of hygiene, if the kitchen is clean, don't mistake untidy for dirty as it is quite normal during busy service for some level of untidiness but just looking at the chefs and his staffs appearances, whether they look personally clean and hygienic. Fridges and kitchen storage should always be tidy, clean and well maintained. You should never feel under estimated by any of your staff and your involvement in your business because at the end of the day it is your business. Now a days it is common practice to have customer satisfaction fill in cards on the tables and it is well worth taking the time every now and then to read them, if they are not available in your restaurant I would strongly suggest you start using them as it will give you a very good idea whether or not your customers are getting what they really want and are paying good money for, and it will give you a fair idea if these people went away happy and will return again and better still if they would recommend your establishment to others. If not you will know when and where changes need to be made. The ambiance needs to be relaxed and at ease but if the kitchen staff us not running smoothly this will reflect on the floor staff and service often causing delay in service which is one of the most annoying things for a customer. If food is being returned on a regular basis where customers are not happy with what they have been served its time to pull the head chef aside and decide his future in your establishment. For every unhappy customer that leaves your restaurant it's a certain unwanted feeling they have taken away with them which is going to lead to them speaking badly about their experience to others which will lead to people who may have been thinking to dine in your restaurant taking their custom else where and be sure you will never see an unhappy customer again. Remember the loss in a booking is not a loss for the chefs pocket it is you that is losing out as you still have to pay the staff, electricity, gas and other costs of running a restaurant, even when the return in profits are practically nil for you. The chef and manager still have to be there and they know this and know they will be paid at the end of the week whether you made money or not so the crooked ones think to themselves 'well why should I knock myself out working as I know I will get paid at the end of the week and I will have my special rewards from the suppliers at the end of the month'. If percentages are high and gross profits match up and balance between the purchase and sale of food then you know maybe its time to start trusting them. If there is a separate bar to the restaurant in your establishment, make it clear and set down strong outlined rules that the bar staff do not fine dine during their shifts in return for the head chefs and managers to drink from a free bar at night. That's why surprise visits to your establishment is highly recommended.

I have already told you a shocking story of one owner falling in to bad debt at the hands of his chef, if you do not want to follow his path you as the owner need to keep your ear to the ground at all times and get to know your staff at all levels. As long as the managers with their muppet deputies are parading around in their suits looking important pretending to be doing something, that's all that matters to them. In hotels its always the same scenario, you have the general manager, assistant general manager, duty manager, bar manager assistant manager, marketing manager, head receptionist her assistant, so all these personnel to practically do f**k all because its not in their job description, or put it this way are not there to actually work but delegate to the few at the bottom, as the old saying goes 'too many generals not enough soldiers on the battle ship'. One person hands over the days schedules to the next from the managers to the deputies to their assistants from one department to another and you will find somewhere along the chain some of them are robbing you as I explained earlier. At the end of the day in a lot of cases there is not enough money to pay all these un-needed staff, so there is no option but to close the doors. This can be avoided by making cuts right from the top. If you the owner want to keep your doors open and also make money you need to be involved in your business, cut out all the over paid un-needed middlemen then you will feel the touch of reality. Carrying weight around will only make you tired. Starting from all heads of departments check your weekly lodgings, visit your kitchen on a regular basis, you might get the shock of your life, your surprise visits will start making your staff pay attention to their responsibilities. The presence of the higher authority will make all the staff take their duties seriously if enforced properly. In most hotels I have worked in, it was very rare to see the owner about, whether they think they are too important or else they are thinking they have employed certain people to run or manage it for them but unfortunately this does not always happen. When on the rare occasion the owner does turn up you will be guaranteed to see all the managers and their muppet deputies in toe running around like headless chickens, clutching folders running from department to department making themselves look like they are working tirelessly and under severe pressure, trying to squeeze a bit of sweat out of themselves. They are running around corridors with loud voices, pretending to be giving orders and showing like ' yeah I am showing people what to do and directing operations'. What a bunch of losers. Then you have the people answering the phones at the reception, they are some good actors too when the owner is around, answering the phones like everything is rosy in the garden, speaking in the perfect tone of manner, hello or good morning, this is the xxxxxxxx hotel how can I help you, yes sir/madam of course that's no problem and the c**p continues all for the owners benefit and he will think she is doing a wonderful job. S**t she is doing a great job. If the owner had not been there the scenario would have been a lot different. The phone would ring and ring and ring until she was finished having the conversation she was engaged in bitching about one of her colleagues. Eventually out of breath she will answer the phone only because it is annoying her. Her greeting to the caller will be a lot different to when the owner was about, something like, Hello xxxxxxxx hotel, yes what are you looking for there will be no mention of sir or madam no nice tone of manner, because all she wants to do is get back to the conversation she was having prior to the phone call she really didn't want to answer. Customers lose faith and trust in an establishment when the staff show such a lack of ability or capability to do their job losing the establishment custom, and it's the owner who is at loss once again. If the proper guidelines and instructions are not put in place by qualified personnel in each department it will just lead to disaster for both the owner and the customer. Small but rational, if the chef serves good meals and the waiting staff serve it with a smile then half the battles won, after all that's what they are being paid to do, serve the people, who at the end of the day are actually paying their wages, without them the place would be closed down.

Owners I am reaching out to you with my knowledge of kitchens and hotel operations in the hope of helping you not to fall in to the debt trap been laid down for you by your staff. Keep your establishment open, running smoothly with good reviews and making a nice earning for you.

As I said this is not a book about learning to cook but I will leave you with this recipe that crooked chefs use to cook your books with the help of suppliers.

Butcher	£200
Fishman	£100
Dry goods	£200
Fruit and veg	£50
	———
Weekly total	£550

When you combine this mixture in a bowl you get a very nice financial mixture for the chef in fact a £550 mixture.

The bigger the order the bigger the weekly pudding.

So when your bread and butter pudding, if you are with me is being cooked it is only shrinking never rising and believe me you will never have the cherry on top.